MW00891861

ISBN: 978-1-956462-79-1
Edition: March 2022

For all inquiries, please contact us at:
info@puppysmiles.org

To see more of our books, visit us at:
www.PuppyDogsAndIceCream.com

Foreward

by Dr. Curtis Hsia

I like it when my kids try new things like jumping into the deep end of the pool or letting a spider crawl across their hands at the park. Sometimes their "what if's" get in the way: "What if I can't swim in the deep end? What if the spider bites me?". My job is to help them think through their fears and help them "get comfortable being uncomfortable."

This book is about a kid learning that having worrying thoughts doesn't mean he can't have fun - doing fun things despite his scary thoughts, not avoiding things because of his fears. Trying things despite scary emotions and thoughts is the basis for the work I do as a doctor in Cognitive Behavioral Therapy.

Dr. Curtis Hsia earned his doctorate in clinical psychology, specializing in Anxiety and Obsessive-Compulsive Disorders. He has published in scientific journals and regularly gives workshops and lectures internationally. He was a fellow at the Center for Anxiety and related disorders at Boston University, an associate professor at Azusa Pacific University and is currently the director at the OC Anxiety Center in Southern California.

This book is given with love...

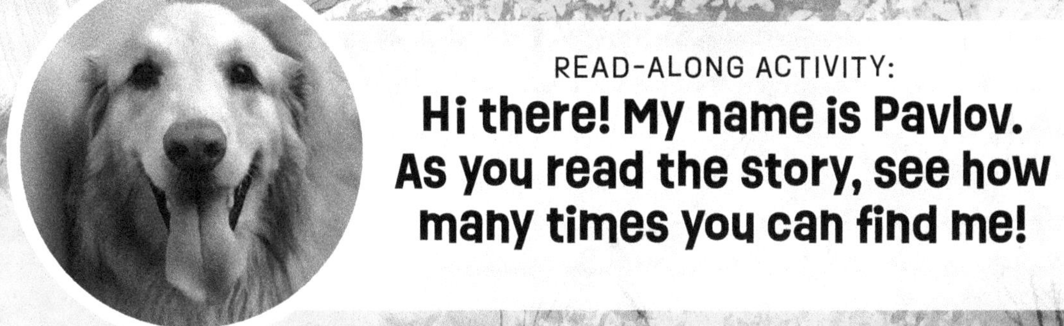

Thomas stood in his backyard and stared up at the giant oak tree.
He was bored and wanted to do something fun, but what?

Then he had a brain blast!
"I'm going to build a tree house!" Thomas declared.

Thomas knew that if he had a tree house, lots of friends would come over to play. They could have secret clubhouse meetings, sleepovers on the weekend, and pretend to be pirates protecting hidden treasure.

The fun would never end if only he had a tree house!

So, Thomas wandered over to the shed and pulled out his trusty red wagon to help with the big job ahead.

Thomas then ran to the hardware store with his trusty red wagon squeaking behind him.

When Thomas entered the hardware store,
the store clerk greeted Thomas with a curious smile.

"Can I help you?" the clerk asked
"I'm going to build a tree house!" Thomas declared.
"Sounds like a lot of fun," said the clerk.
**"You'll need some wood, a hammer, nails, glue, a saw,
a tape measure, and a rope ladder."**

Thomas carefully picked out everything he needed and piled it into his trusty red wagon. He paid the clerk almost all of his allowance and said, **"Thank you for helping."** Thomas left, excited, with a wagon full of supplies.

He ran home with a smile on his face, and his
trusty red wagon squeaking behind him.

GLUE

When Thomas got home, he took the supplies out of his wagon and started to organize everything into piles. He then looked up at the big oak tree and suddenly had the scariest, most terrible, horrible, thoughts!

"What if the tree house looks silly?"

"What if the rope ladder suddenly breaks, and we get stuck in the tree house?"

"What if a family of squirrels takes over the tree house to store all their nuts inside?"

"What if no one wants to play in the tree house with me?"

"What if my tree house is a GIANT disaster?"

Thomas decided he couldn't take any chances. It was better to not build the tree house at all. He pushed his supplies aside and spent the rest of the day wishing he had something fun to do.

The next day, Thomas was sitting in the backyard watching a plane go by, when he had another brain blast!

"I'm going to build a rocket!" Thomas declared.

Thomas knew that if he had a rocket, lots of friends would come over to play. They could shoot up into space and visit the Moon, Mars or discover new planets, and meet three-eyed aliens!

The fun would never end if only he had a rocket!

So, he grabbed his trusty red wagon to help with the big job ahead. Thomas ran to the craft store with his trusty red wagon squeaking behind him.

When Thomas entered the craft store, the store clerk came over and smiled.

"Can I help you?" the clerk asked.

"I'm going to build a model rocket!" Thomas declared.

"Well, that sounds like more fun than a barrel of monkeys!" said the clerk.

"You'll need some tubes, glue, buttons, string, fuses, levers, and switches. Plus, you'll probably want a tiny space-man to put inside."

Thomas carefully picked out everything he needed and piled it into his trusty red wagon. He gave the clerk the rest of his allowance, thanked her for her help, and headed home.

He walked home with a smile on his face, and his trusty red wagon squeaking behind him.

When Thomas got home, he took the supplies out of his wagon and started to organize everything into piles. He then looked up at the big, blue sky and suddenly had the scariest, most terrible, horrible thoughts.

"What if the rocket doesn't even take off?"

"What if it goes right into the tree and gets stuck there forever?"

"What if the rocket takes us to a strange planet with slimy aliens?"

"What if everyone sees my rocket fail and laughs at me?"

"What if my model rocket is a GIANT disaster?"

Thomas decided he couldn't take any chances. It was better not to build the rocket at all. He pushed his supplies aside and spent the rest of the day wishing he had something fun to do.

The next day, Thomas was sitting
in the backyard wishing he had
something fun to do. Unfortunately,
he didn't have any money left...
He had spent all his allowance.
That's when Thomas had another
brain blast!

"I'm going to build a lemonade stand!" Thomas declared. Thomas knew that if he had a lemonade stand, he would have money for his next big project.

He could create a sign as big as his house so people could see it from far away. He could wave at all the neighbors who drove by and make the lemonade all different colors of the rainbow so people could pick their favorite.

The fun would never end if only he had a lemonade stand!

So, he grabbed his trusty red wagon to help with the big job ahead. Thomas marched into the house with his trusty red wagon squeaking behind him.

Thomas headed into the kitchen with his wagon, where his mom was cleaning out the cupboards.

"Hi Thomas!" his mom said, **"What's the plan for today?"**

"I'm going to build a lemonade stand!" Thomas declared.

"How fun! I loved making lemonade stands when I was your age," said his mom. **"You'll need a tablecloth, a sign, cups, pitchers, napkins, sugar, lemons, water, ice, a chair to sit on, and an umbrella for shade to stay cool."**

Thomas and his mom gathered all the supplies he needed and placed them carefully into his trusty wagon. He thanked his mom for her help, and went out to the front of his house, with a smile on his face, and his trusty red wagon squeaking behind him.

Thomas picked out the perfect spot on the corner of his street. He took his supplies out of his wagon and started to organize everything into piles. He then looked out at the big, busy road and suddenly had the scariest, most terrible, horrible thoughts.

"What if I don't sell any lemonade?"

"What if it rains, and the lemonade stand gets ruined?"

"What if my lemonade attracts a hive of bees who carry the stand away to their queen?"

"What if my lemonade tastes like a stinky pair of old socks?"

"What if my lemonade stand is a GIANT disaster?"

Thomas decided he couldn't take any chances. It was better not to build the lemonade stand at all. He pushed his supplies aside and spent the rest of the day wishing he had something fun to do.

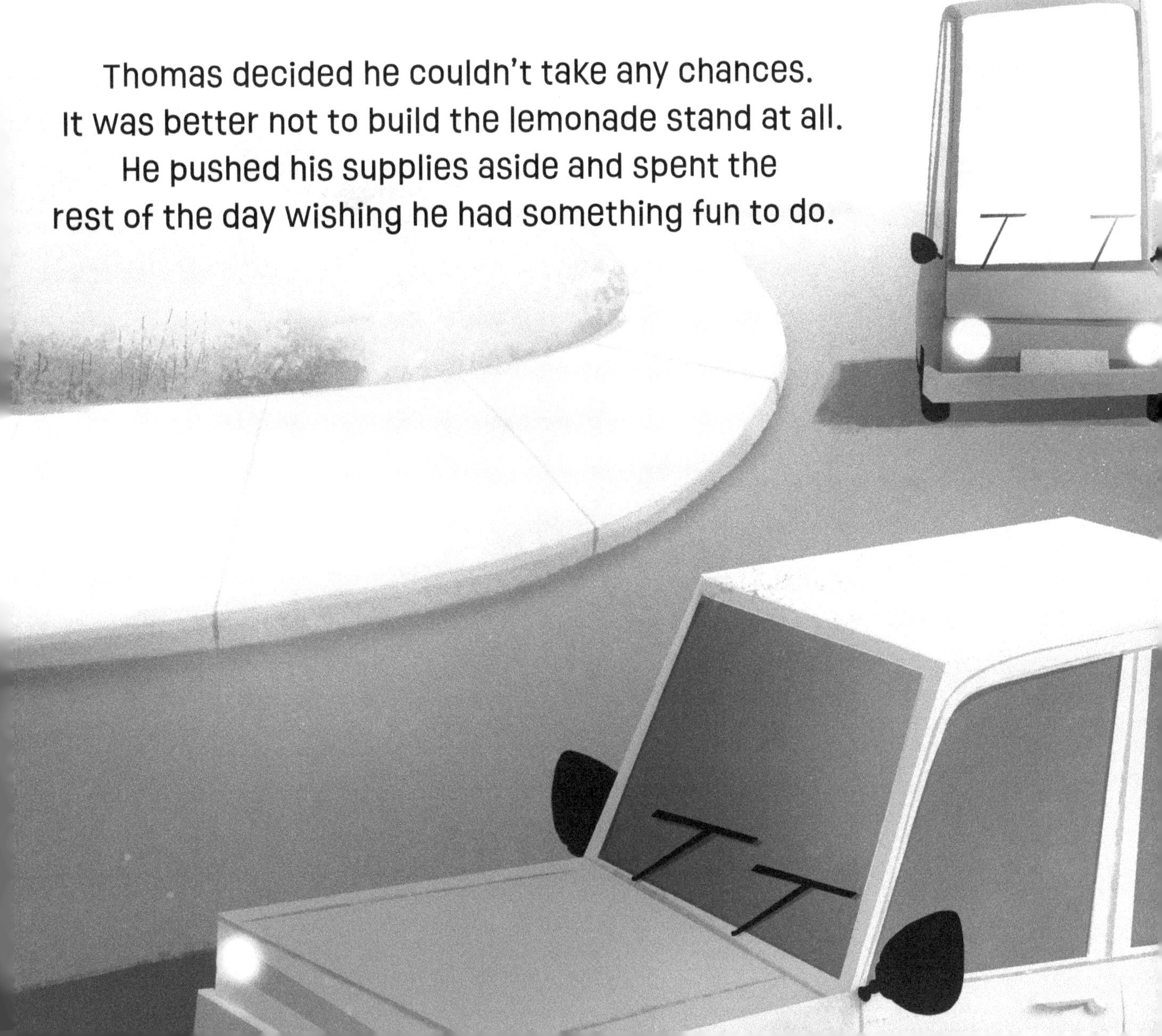

Thomas looked up and saw his neighbor Angie pulling her old blue wagon with the wobbly wheel.

"Hi Thomas!" she called out. **"What do you have there?"**

"It's a lemonade stand, but I don't want to build it anymore," Thomas mumbled, looking at the ground and kicking at the grass.

"A lemonade stand? That sounds like so much fun!" Angie said, **"Can I have it?"**

Thomas shrugged. He had already given up on his lemonade stand, so he might as well give it to Angie.

"Sure," shrugged Thomas. **"I've got a tablecloth, a sign, cups, pitchers, napkins, sugar, lemons, water, ice, a chair, and an umbrella for shade to stay cool."**

"Thank you, Thomas!" Angie exclaimed, **"This is going to be so much fun! Do you want to build it with me?"**

Thomas shook his head. **"No thanks. I don't know how to build it, and it will probably turn out badly."**

Thomas carefully placed all the lemonade stand supplies into Angie's old blue wagon. Angie headed home with a smile on her face and her old blue wagon wobbling behind her.

Thomas went to the backyard and looked at the big pile of rocket supplies. Now that he gave Angie the lemonade stand, he wanted to get rid of the rocket stuff too.

After all, it might never even take off. Thomas looked up and saw his neighbor Jacob pulling his rusty green wagon with the clunky wheel.

"Hi Thomas!" he waved. **"What do you have there?'**

"It's a rocket, but I don't want to build it anymore," Thomas sighed.

"Wow, fun! I've always wanted to build a rocket!"
Jacob asked, **"Can I have it?"**

"Sure," said Thomas. **"I've got tubes, glue, buttons, string, fuses, levers, and switches. Plus, you'll probably want a tiny space-man to put inside."**

"Wow, thanks, Thomas!" Jacob exclaimed.
"This is going to be so much fun!
Do you want to build it with me?"

Thomas responded shyly, **"No thanks. I don't know how to build it, and it probably won't work."**

Thomas carefully placed all the model rocket supplies into Jacob's rusty green wagon. Jacob headed home with a smile on his face and his rusty green wagon wobbling behind him.

The next day, Thomas decided to go visit Angie and see if she did anything with the lemonade stand. When he arrived at Angie's house, he saw the lemonade stand all set up, and Angie was sitting on the chair, under the umbrella to stay cool.

"Wow Angie, this looks so cool!" Thomas said. **"But weren't you nervous?"**

"About what?" Angie asked.

"What if you don't sell any lemonade?" Thomas asked.

"What if it rains, and the lemonade gets ruined?"

"What if your lemonade attracts a hive of bees who carry the stand away to their queen?"

"What if your lemonade tastes like a stinky pair of old socks?"

"What if your lemonade stand is a GIANT disaster?"

"Well, I haven't sold any lemonade yet," Angie shrugged,

"But that's OK... I just did it to have fun," Angie said smiling.

Angie continued, **"My first cup was so sweet my tongue was tingling.**

My second cup was so sour my eyes nearly popped out. But, my third cup was perfect!"

"Thomas, do you want to try a cup?"
Thomas took a sip of the lemonade, and it was delicious!

"Oh, this is really good lemonade!" said Thomas. **"Are you having fun?"**

"Yes, I'm having lots of fun!" Angie laughed, **"and I'm glad you like the lemonade."**

"I had fun mixing all the ingredients, decorating the stand, and I'm having fun waving to the neighbors!

"Even if I don't sell any lemonade, that means I get to drink it," said Angie giggling. **"Thank you for giving me all the supplies!"**

"You're welcome," said Thomas, **"Thank you for the lemonade."**

Thomas walked away, smiling and sipping his lemonade. Maybe he was too hasty when he gave up on his lemonade stand?

Later that afternoon, Thomas decided to go visit Jacob and see if he did anything with the rocket. When Thomas arrived at Jacob's house, he saw the rocket all set up, ready for launch.

"Wow Jacob, this looks so cool!" Thomas said.
"But weren't you scared?"

"Scared of what?" Jacob asked.

"What if the rocket doesn't even launch?" Thomas asked.

"What if it goes right into a big oak tree and gets stuck there forever?"

"What if the rocket takes you to a strange planet with slimy aliens?"

"What if everyone sees your rocket fail and laughs at you?"

"What if your rocket is a GIANT disaster?"

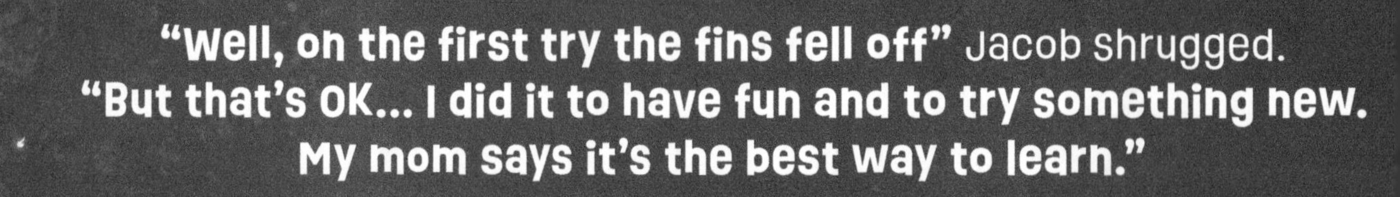

"Well, on the first try the fins fell off" Jacob shrugged. **"But that's OK... I did it to have fun and to try something new. My mom says it's the best way to learn."**

"Oh," said Thomas. **"Are you having fun? Did you learn anything?"**

"I'm having lots of fun!" Jacob laughed. **"I had fun putting all the pieces together, decorating the rocket, and I'm having fun checking the wires."**

"Even if the rocket doesn't fly, I've learned so much already. Thank you for giving me the supplies, Thomas!"

"You're welcome," Thomas said, **"Good luck with your rocket!"**

Thomas walked away, imagining all the fun Jacob was having. Maybe he was worrying too much when he gave up on the rocket?

Thomas decided to head home, but he couldn't stop thinking about Angie and Jacob...

They weren't scared of giant disasters. They just wanted to try something new to share with others, learn, and have fun!

Thomas thought about how it wasn't until Angie's third try that her lemonade turned out delicious. He thought about how Jacob wasn't worried the rocket might not launch at all.

Thomas had to admit, even if Angie didn't sell a single cup of lemonade, and even if Jacob couldn't get his rocket off the ground, it looked like they were having a blast!

Thomas went to his room and stared at the pile of tree house supplies...

He realized that even if he didn't build the world's greatest tree house, it might be worth a try!

Thomas thought about all the scary thoughts that had been stopping him before.

"What if the tree house looks silly?"
He would still have fun being the king of his own amazing tree house!

"What if the rope ladder suddenly breaks, and we get stuck in the tree house?"
The rope ladder he bought is strong enough to hold up an elephant. As long as no more than one elephant tries to climb into his tree house, he would be safe!

"What if a family of squirrels take over the tree house to store all their nuts inside?"
Then he could have fun pets that could be the mascots of the tree house. He could bring them all sorts of nuts, and they would scare away spiders.

"What if no one wants to play in the tree house with me?"
Then it would become his own secret hide-away. If people did want to play in the tree house later, Thomas could make a secret password to enter!

"What if my tree house is a GIANT disaster?"
How could it be a GIANT disaster when it would be so much fun to design, build, decorate, and play in his very own tree house?

With a look of determination, Thomas decided he didn't want to wait any longer for the fun to start!

Thomas got to work.

He took the wood and
tape measure up the tree with his
saw, hammer, nails, and glue.

Thomas started to build his tree house.

He did have a little bit of trouble attaching
the ladder. He did encounter a couple of squirrels,
but he was having so much fun that nothing would
stop Thomas from completing his tree house!

**After a few hours, Thomas hammered in the
last nail and climbed down the rope ladder
which held him strong and steady.**

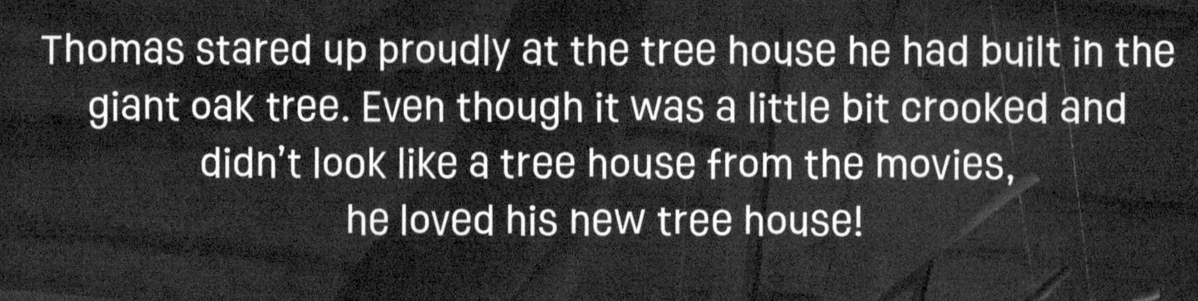

Thomas stared up proudly at the tree house he had built in the giant oak tree. Even though it was a little bit crooked and didn't look like a tree house from the movies, he loved his new tree house!

Thomas had a lot of fun building the tree house, and his rope ladder was more than strong enough to go up and down safely. When he told Angie and Jacob about his new tree house, they couldn't wait to come play in it.

"Your tree house is awesome!" they both said when they saw it for the first time. Thomas was proud of his hard work. The tree house didn't look exactly how Thomas had imagined, but still, the three of them had the best day ever!

They had decorated the tree house, fed the squirrels, pretended to be pirates, and even created a secret password.

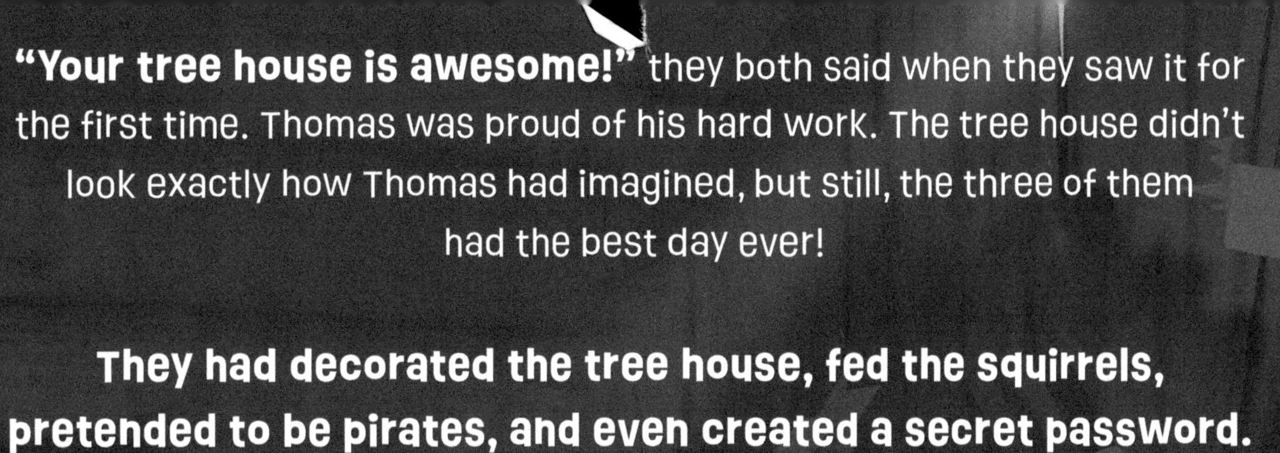

Even though trying something new made him worry, Thomas realized that these worried thoughts don't always come true, and trying was totally worth it in the end! He learned that things don't have to be perfect, and his fear of failing had been holding him back from having fun all along.

Thomas decided to choose fun over fear.
As it turned out, all Thomas had to do was try!

CPSIA information can be obtained
at www.ICGtesting.com
Printed in the USA
BVHW062247280922
648142BV00009B/102